# Little
# HORRORS

## Shiver with fear...

Owwl!

## ...shake with laughter!

For Adam and Vincent

Leabharlanna Chuntai Phortláirge

Visit Shoo Rayner's website!
www.shoo-rayner.co.uk

J/1931449

ORCHARD BOOKS
96 Leonard Street, London EC2A 4XD
*Orchard Books Australia*
Unit 31/56 O'Riordan Street, Alexandria, NSW 2015
First published in Great Britain in 2002
First paperback edition 2002
Copyright © Shoo Rayner 2002
The right of Shoo Rayner to be identified as the author
and illustrator of this work has been asserted by him in
accordance with the Copyright, Designs, and Patents Act, 1988.
A CIP catalogue record for this book is available
from the British Library.
ISBN 1 84121 642 9 (hardback)
ISBN 1 84121 650 X (paperback)
1 3 5 7 9 10 8 6 4 2 (hardback)
1 3 5 7 9 10 8 6 4 2 (paperback)
Printed in Great Britain

# Little
# HORRORS
## The Sand Man

ORCHARD BOOKS

I could hardly breathe.

"H-help!" I gasped. "This tree is trying to s-s-strangle me!"

"Don't be stupid!" laughed my
sister, Kim, as she untangled the
branches from around my neck.

Soon I had wriggled free.

"This place gives me the creeps," I said, my legs still shaking with fright. But Kim wasn't listening to me.

A brambly path led from the top of the cliff, down to a small, sandy cove. "Race you!" Kim yelled, and we both scrambled to the ground.

Kim and I
chased each other
along the path...

...all the way down to the beach.

It was fantastic.

As we dug into the soft sand, a
long, dark shadow loomed over us.

It was an old man.

His face was brown and wrinkled, like the bark of a tree.

"There's not many people brave enough to come down to Sand Man's beach," the old man said.

He went on in his dry, crackly voice, "You be sure not to take any sand away from here, now."

Then he pointed his walking-stick
towards the tree on top of the cliff.

"Folk round here call *him* the
Sand Man."

Fear trickled down my spine like grains of sand. The tree we'd been climbing, the tree that had tried to strangle me, was…

…the Sand Man!

The old man kept his eyes on us.
They glittered in the sunlight.

Staying up at the campsite are you?

"If you take any sand from the beach," he told us, "be sure to leave it outside your tent at night."

With a toothy grin, the old man whispered, "Be warned!"

Sand Man always gets his way!

Then he shuffled off. His long, dark shadow trailed behind him.

Back at the campsite, we told Mum
and Dad all about the Sand Man.

"You can't beat an old sailor for telling stories!" said Dad. Then he chased us round and round the tent.

At bedtime, we shook every single grain of sand from our towels and swimming costumes.

We swept it into a jar, and left it outside the tent.

I snuggled down into my sleeping bag, thinking about the Sand Man.

Was it just a silly story?

Would he *really* come for his sand?

And, what would happen if one night, he didn't find it?

Finally, I drifted off to sleep.
But *something*
woke me up
with a jump.

I could hear bony
fingers scratching
at the tent flaps.

*Something* was trying to get in!

23

The next morning, the jar was
lying on its side.

The sand had all gone!

Kim glanced up at the tree, and gave me a worried look.

D-d-do you believe in the Sand Man?

Just then, the wind dropped, and the leaves stopped rustling. Was the tree waiting to hear my answer?

"Come on!" I shouted. "Let's go down to the beach!"

Kim and I played on Sand Man's beach every day. And every day, the old man shuffled by.

Every night, we swept up the sand
and left it in the jar.

Every morning, the jar was empty!

On the last day of our holiday, we took my kite down to the beach.

Suddenly, the wind blew stronger and colder.

The sky grew dark.

I could hardly hold onto the kite.

Lightning flashed.

The string snapped, and the kite
hurtled towards the cliffs.

It snagged in the Sand Man.

I could see the kite trying to break free, but the branches wouldn't let it go. The Sand Man had trapped the kite, just like he'd trapped me…

We ran all the way back to the tent, and collapsed on the floor in a cold, wet heap.

Mum made us a hot drink and we snuggled into our sleeping bags.

Dad told us spooky stories until it was time for bed.

It took me ages to fall asleep. I had a feeling we'd forgotten something very important...

I was awake in an instant.

My heart was banging, and my
head was spinning.

What was going on?

"Holey moley!" I heard Dad shout.
"That was close!"

Then, without warning…

…the side of our tent ripped
right open, from top to bottom!

Rain rushed in through the hole,
soaking us to the bone.

Like a dog with a rag, the wind
shook the tent around.

Above the howling and wailing,
I could hear Mum and Dad.

Kim grabbed my hand.
I peeped out into the darkness.

A gigantic bolt of lightning lit up
the sky, and in that split-second
I saw it…

Deep, hollow eyes glared out from an ugly, gnarled face. Long, scratchy fingers reached towards the tent, clawing at the air.

Then I remembered…

"Kim!" I croaked. "We forgot to sweep up the sand last night!"

We looked at each other.

Then everything went crazy.

The wind whipped round the tent,
tearing it to shreds. Kim and I
stumbled about, blinded by sand...

...until Dad led us safely to the car.

We stayed there all night.

Early the next morning, as we were getting ready to drive home, the old man appeared.

I see the Sand Man got his way, then!

He nodded towards the tree.

Glinting in its
branches was
the jar. *It was
full of sand!*

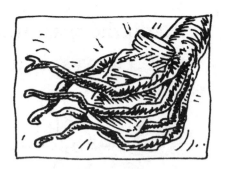

The old man chuckled loudly, and
I began to wonder...

Had *he* emptied the jar every night?
Had *he* put the jar in the tree?
Before I could ask, the old man
had vanished.

I looked back at the tree. Its
rustling leaves seemed to whisper...

The Sand Man always gets his way!

### Little Horrors by Shoo Rayner

| | | |
|---|---|---|
| ❑ The Swamp Man | 1 84121 646 1 | £3.99 |
| ❑ The Pumpkin Man | 1 84121 644 5 | £3.99 |
| ❑ The Spider Man | 1 84121 648 8 | £3.99 |
| ❑ The Sand Man | 1 84121 650 X | £3.99 |

### Finger Clicking Reads by Shoo Rayner

| | | |
|---|---|---|
| ❑ Rock-a-doodle-do! | 1 84121 465 5 | £3.99 |
| ❑ Treacle, Treacle, Little Tart | 1 84121 469 8 | £3.99 |

### Grandpa Turkey's Tall Tales by Jonathan Allen

| | | |
|---|---|---|
| ❑ King of the Birds | 1 84121 877 4 | £3.99 |
| ❑ And Pigs Might Fly | 1 84121 710 7 | £3.99 |

### The One and Only by Laurence Anholt and Tony Ross

| | | |
|---|---|---|
| ❑ Micky the Muckiest Boy | 1 86039 983 5 | £3.99 |
| ❑ Ruby the Rudest Girl | 1 86039 623 2 | £3.99 |
| ❑ Harold the Hairiest Man | 1 86039 624 0 | £3.99 |

*And many more!*